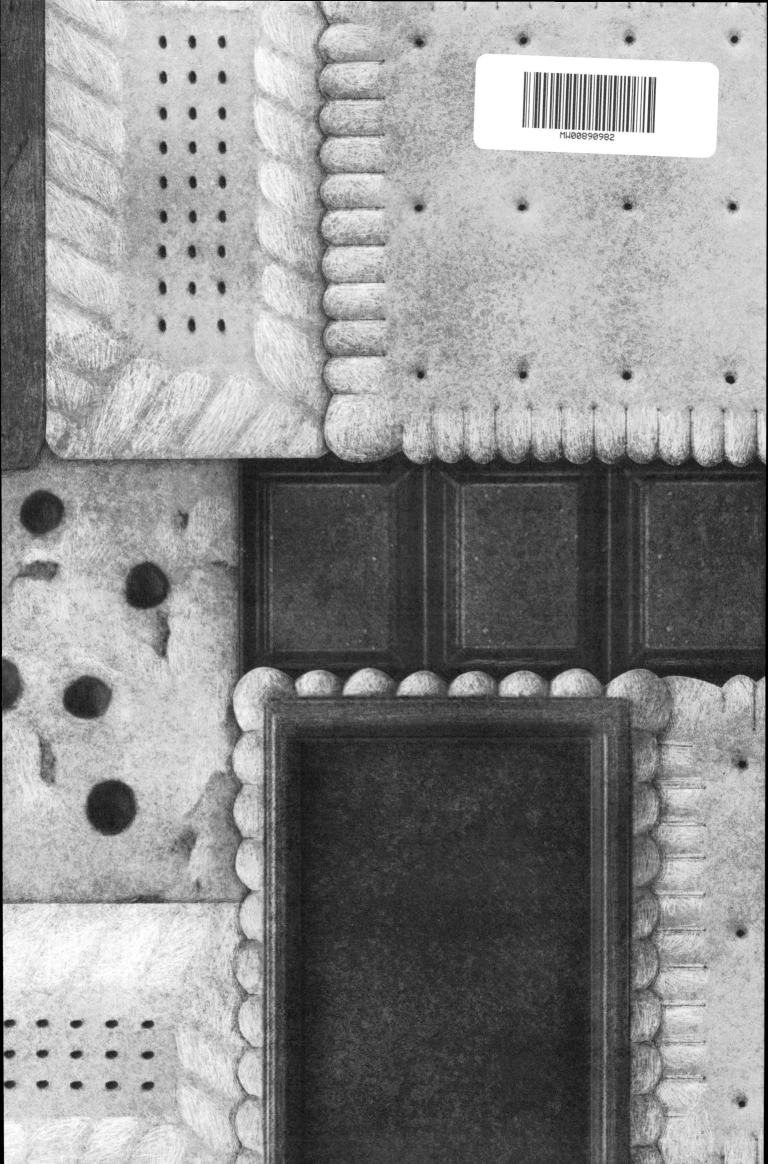

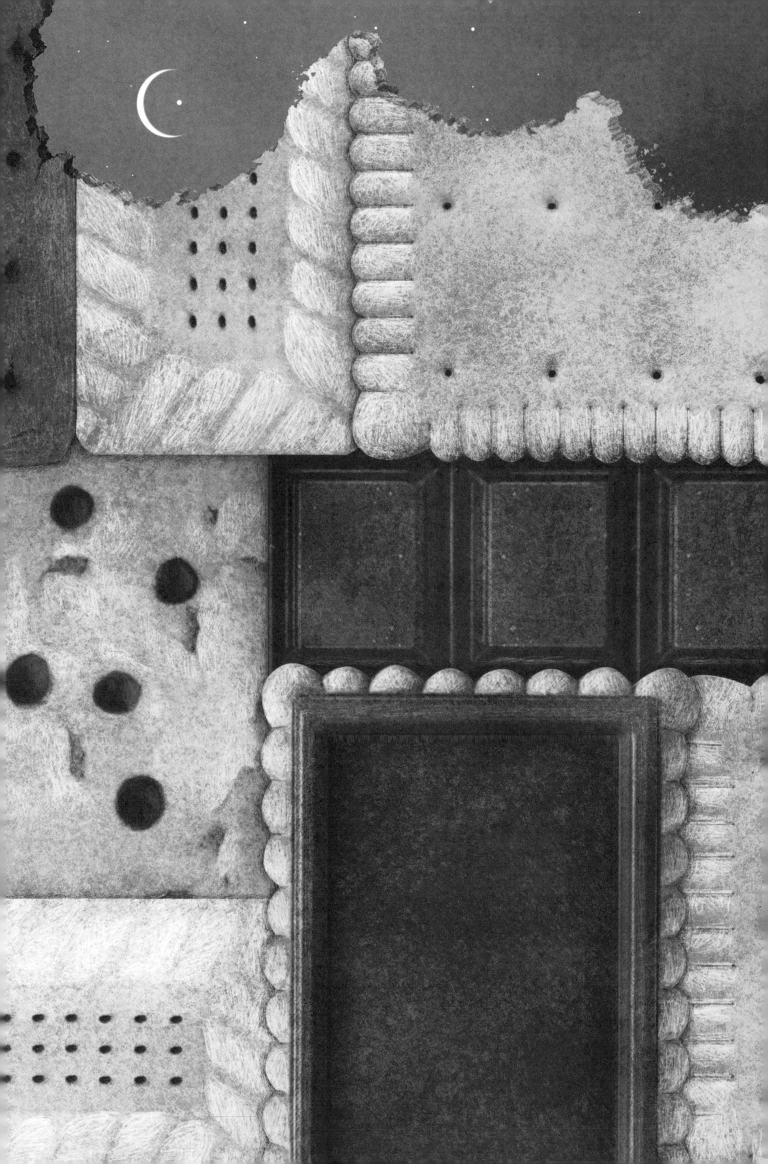

HaNSeL aNd GreteL

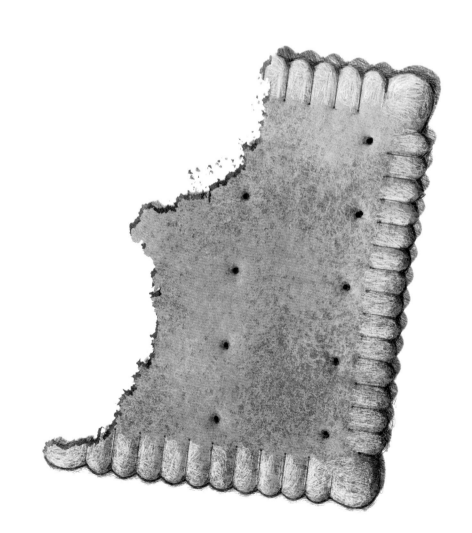

From a fairy tale by the
BrotHers Grimm

Illustrations by
FranceSca coSanti

WSKids
WHITE STAR KIDS

On the edge of a great forest lived a woodcutter who was so poor
that he had nothing to feed his family. He could hardly even buy
bread for his wife and his two children, Hansel and Gretel.

One evening, his wife said to him, "Husband of mine, we cannot
go on like this. Tomorrow morning at dawn, take the children
into the forest, then, when they are playing, leave them there."

The man exclaimed sadly, "Wife of mine, I cannot bring myself
to leave my children alone in the forest!"

The wife would not change her mind and she insisted until the
poor man agreed. The two children were so hungry that they could
not sleep and they heard their parents talking. Gretel began to cry,
but Hansel said, "Little sister, don't worry. I have a plan."

Without making a sound, the boy got up, put on his jacket
and went outside. The moon was bright and the white pebbles
glittered like new silver pennies. Hansel picked up a handful
and hid them in his pockets. Then he went inside and slept
quietly. At dawn, their mother woke them, saying cheerfully,
"Get up, today we are going into the forest." All along the path,
Hansel dropped the white pebbles, one after another.

When they reached the center of the forest, the father lit
a fire and the mother said, "Now, lie down and rest for a while.
We are going to chop some wood in the forest.
Be good and don't go far. We will be back soon."

Hansel and Gretel waited a long time for their parents to come
and get them. When night fell, Gretel began to cry, but her brother
said, "Don't cry. We just have to wait for the moon to rise."

When the moon rose, Hansel took Gretel by the
hand. The pebbles shone under the light of the moon,
showing them the way.

When they arrived home, it was already morning.

Their father was happy to see them home safely, but their mother was furious.
Soon she convinced her husband to abandon the children in the forest once again.

Again, Hansel overheard the conversation and as soon as it was dark, he got out of bed and quietly went to gather some pebbles. Unfortunately, the door of the house was locked and he couldn't go outside.

He didn't want to frighten Gretel, so he went back to bed without telling her anything, but he didn't sleep, he spent all night thinking of a new plan to save himself and his little sister.

When the sun rose, the mother gave
the children a piece of bread for breakfast.
Along the path, Hansel dropped crumbs
of bread, step after step, to mark the way.
When they reached the forest, the parents
told the children to lie down and rest,
promising to return and fetch them before
the evening.

Night fell, but no one came to fetch them. Hansel comforted Gretel, saying, "Wait for the moon to rise, then we can see the crumbs of bread that I dropped and find our way home."

The moon rose, but when Hansel looked for the crumbs, he couldn't find them. The little birds of the forest had eaten them all!

Hansel and Gretel walked all night and all the next day, looking for the path to home, but they just went further into the forest. They were so tired, disheartened and hungry that, in the end, they lay down and fell into a deep sleep.

On the third day, they found a strange small house,
made of biscuits and marzipan, with sugar-glass windows.
They couldn't believe their eyes! They were so hungry that
they couldn't resist temptation, but when Gretel began
to nibble a little piece of the door, a thin voice called out
from inside, "Who is eating my sugar house?"

The door opened suddenly and a wrinkled old woman came out, shaking her head. She said, "How did you get here? Come inside, you are very welcome!"

The hungry children stepped into the house, but as soon as the door closed the old woman's kindness vanished!

You must know that, in fact, she was a wicked witch and she used her house made of biscuits and marzipan to attract children who strayed from their parents while playing and got lost in the forest. You can easily imagine how happy she was the brother and sister had arrived; two children at once: what could be better?

The witch grabbed Hansel and shut him in a cage hanging from the ceiling of the room and then she said to Gretel, "Go into the kitchen and make something good for your brother. I want to fatten him up before I eat him."

Every day Hansel was forced to eat and eat, and every evening the witch went over to the cage and said, "Let me feel your finger, I want to know if you are getting fat."

Hansel had understood what she intended to do, and he had noticed that she could not see very well anymore, so . . . instead of sticking his finger through the bars of the cage, he held out a chicken bone that he had saved.

The old woman, who did not realise his trick, was amazed that he had not become any plumper since he arrived. One evening, tired of waiting, she said to Gretel, "Fat or thin, tomorrow I will roast your brother."

The little girl cried all night, trying in vain to hatch a plan to overcome the witch and save Hansel.

The next morning, when she went into the kitchen, the witch had already lit the fire and she was kneading bread dough before cooking poor Hansel. When she saw Gretel, she said politely, "Look into the oven, lean well in and tell me if the bread in there is baked." In fact, she intended to push Gretel into the oven, roast her and gobble her down!

The child had understood her intentions
and she said, "I can't see to the back
of the oven!"

Impatiently, the old woman leaned
forward and looked into the oven. Quickly
the little girl gave her a hard shove and she
fell inside. Gretel slammed the door shut.

Gretel ran to free her brother. She handed the key of the cage to Hansel and he opened it, jumping to the ground with a big smile. The children hugged each other. They couldn't wait to leave that terrible house, but Hansel decided to take some food for the journey home before they set out. It was a wonderful idea, because when the children pulled the pots and pans down from the shelves, they saw that they were full of precious things: jewels of all kinds shone brightly and there were gold and silver coins that clinked when the children touched them.

The brother and sister picked up everything they
could carry and ran merrily out of the house.
At last they could return home with all that
treasure, they would never be hungry again and they
would live happily ever after.

They walked all day until they came to a clearing that they knew well; in the shadow of the trees, they saw their house! They were not far away, but they did not dare to go closer. Suddenly, the door opened and their father came out. He stared at the edge of the forest, as he had done every day, time after time, since he had abandoned the children. He had left them to please his wife, but now she was dead and he was alone.

When Hansel and Gretel saw him, they ran towards their
father who hugged them joyfully.

Was the long nightmare finally over?

The children excitedly told their father the whole, terrible
story. They were so happy, and he was so extraordinarily happy
to have found them that he would never leave them again!

Francesca Cosanti

Born in Martina Franca (Taranto, Italy) in 1985, she studied Illustration
and Animation Media at the Istituto Europeo di Design (IED) in
Rome, then she attended a course of Illustration at the Accademia
di Illustrazione Officina b5 (Rome) and various intensive courses
with internationally renowned illustrators.
She has worked as an illustrator since 2005 and, at the same time,
she has been teaching in several institutions as expert of illustration
and techniques, graphic design and multimedia software.
In 2007 she won the first prize for the logo of the Presidency of
the Council of Ministers - Department for Community Policies.
She currently works as an illustrator for publishing and advertising,
associations, companies and agencies and, in her spare time, she devotes
herself to her passions: traveling, food, swimming, books, photography
and long walks. In addition to the illustrations found in this book, she
created those for "Little Red Riding Hood" for White Star Kids.

WSkids
WHITE STAR KIDS

White Star Kids® is a registered trademark property of White Star s.r.l.

© 2017 White Star s.r.l.
Piazzale Luigi Cadorna, 6 - 20123 Milan, Italy
www.whitestar.it

Translation: Iceigeo, Milan (Katherine M. Clifton)

ISBN 978-88-544-1186-9
1 2 3 4 5 6   21 20 19 18 17

Printed in China

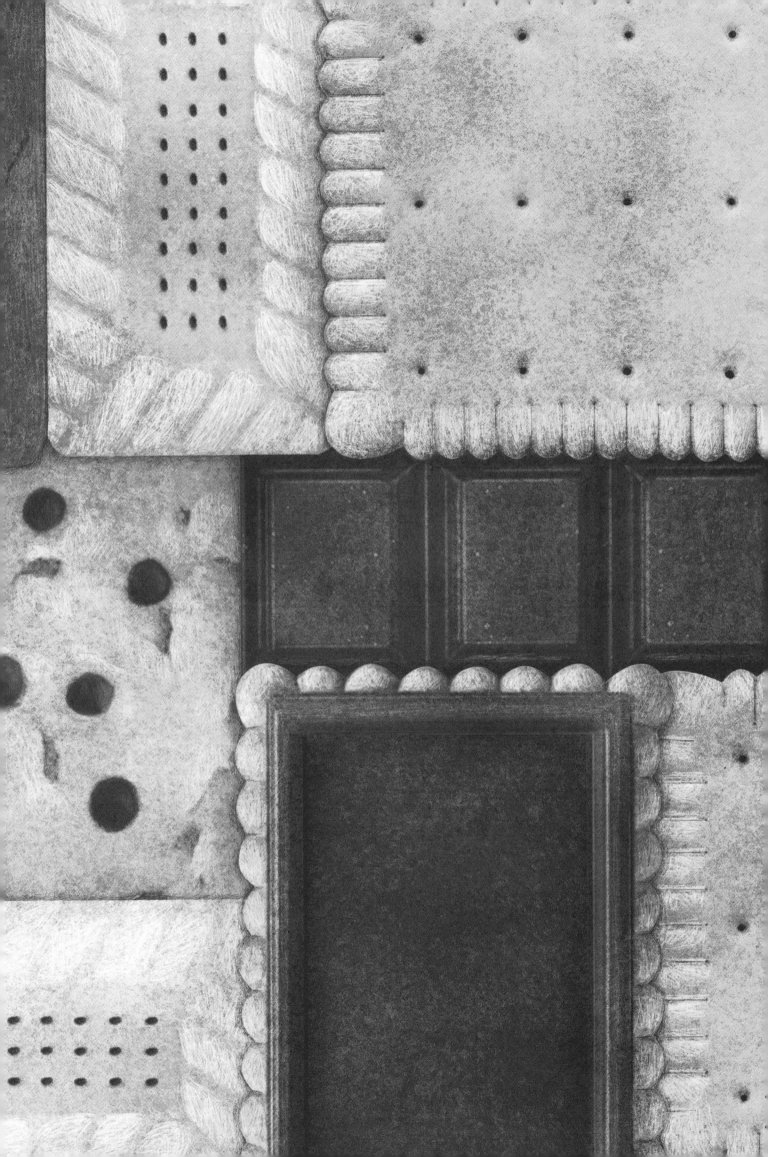